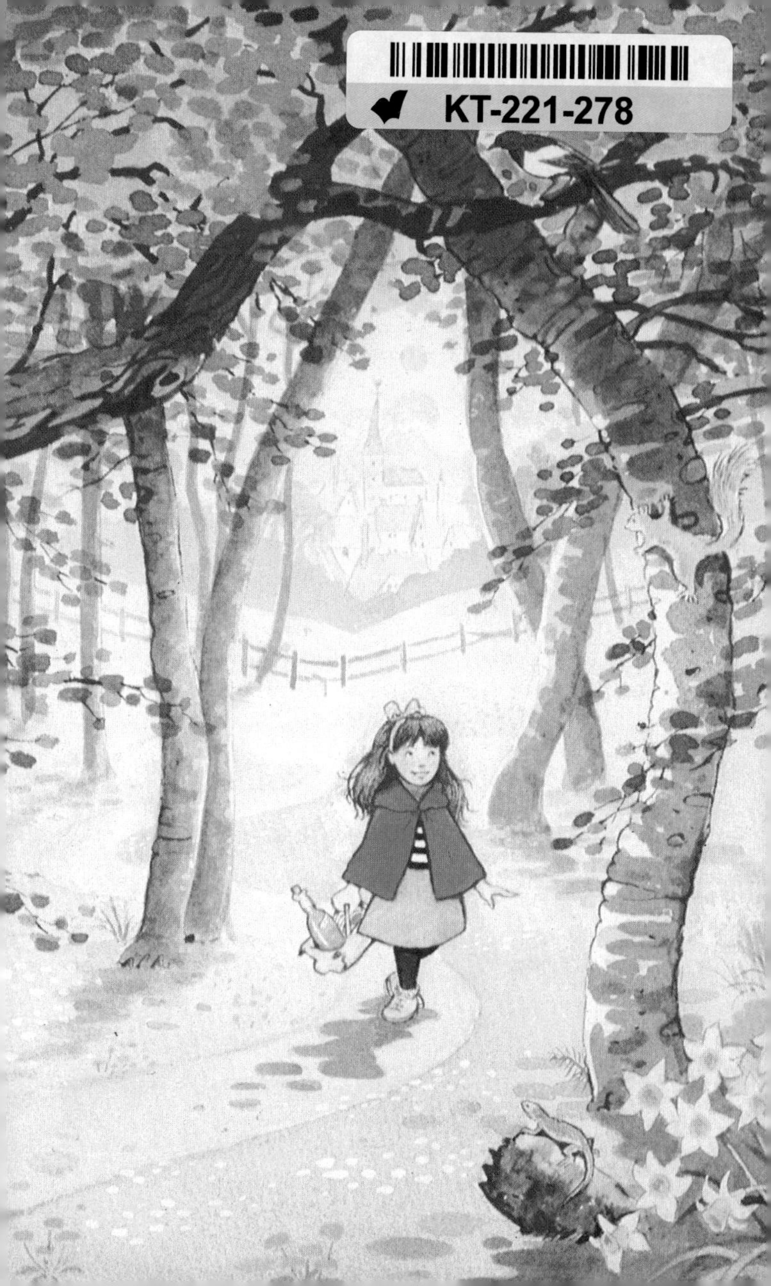

Every new generation of children is enthralled by the famous stories in our Well Loved Tales series. Younger ones love to have the story read to them. Older children will enjoy the exciting stories in an easy-to-read text.

British Library Cataloguing in Publication Data

Southgate, Vera
    Little Red Riding Hood.
    I. Title   II. Stevenson, Peter, *1953-*
823′.914[J]

ISBN 0-7214-1113-4 (Hardback)
ISBN 0-7214-8262-7 (Paperback)

Revised edition

Published by Ladybird Books Ltd Loughborough Leicestershire UK
Ladybird Books Inc Auburn Maine 04210 USA

Printed in England

WELL LOVED TALES

Little Red Riding Hood

retold by VERA SOUTHGATE M A B Com
illustrated by PETER STEVENSON

Ladybird Books

Once upon a time, there was a little girl who was loved by everyone who knew her.

Her grandmother was so fond of the child that she delighted in giving her presents. Once she made her a beautiful cape and hood of red velvet.

The little girl liked it so much that she never went out without wearing it. In time, everyone called her "Little Red Riding Hood".

Little Red Riding Hood lived with her mother and father in a small cottage, in a village, near the edge of a large forest.

Her father worked all day in the forest, as a woodcutter.

Little Red Riding Hood's grandmother lived about a mile away. She lived by herself in a little cottage right inside the wood.

Little Red Riding Hood loved her grandmother, just as much as her grandmother loved her. Nearly every day she went along the path, through the forest, to visit her.

One day Little Red Riding Hood's mother called her and said, "Little Red Riding Hood, I have put a cake and a bottle of wine in this basket. I want you to take them to your grandmother. She is ill and they will do her good.

"Keep to the path and don't wander off into the wood," Little Red Riding Hood's mother warned her.

"Walk carefully and don't run or you may break the bottle. Then you will have no wine for poor Grandmother," went on her mother.

"I shall take great care," promised Little Red Riding Hood, as she took the basket and waved goodbye to her mother.

Before she had gone very far along the path through the forest, Little Red Riding Hood met a wolf.

She had never seen a wolf before and she did not know what a wicked creature he was. She thought he was a large dog and she was not in the least afraid of him.

"Good morning, Little Red Riding Hood," said the wolf.

"Good morning, sir," she replied.

"Where are you going, so early in the morning?" asked the wolf.

"To my grandmother's," she replied.

"And what have you got in your basket?" went on the wolf.

"A cake and a bottle of wine," said Little Red Riding Hood. "Grandmother is ill and Mother has sent these to help her to get well again."

"Where does your grandmother live, Little Red Riding Hood?" continued the wolf.

"About another half mile into the wood," answered Little Red Riding Hood. "Her cottage stands under three large oak trees."

"What a tender young creature this is!" thought the wolf. "She will make a more juicy mouthful than the old woman! But, if I am cunning, I should manage to eat both!"

So the wolf strolled along beside Little Red Riding Hood for a little while, chatting to her and pointing out what was to be seen.

"Look at all the pretty flowers under the trees," he said. "Are they not beautiful? And can you not hear the birds singing? You should stop and enjoy these pleasures instead of walking straight along the path."

Then the wolf said goodbye to Little
Red Riding Hood and set off quickly
for the grandmother's cottage.

Little Red Riding Hood did as the wolf
had suggested and looked around her.
The forest was indeed a lovely place.
The sunbeams danced through the trees,
the ground was carpeted with beautiful
flowers and overhead the birds sang
merrily.

"I shall pick a bunch of fresh flowers for my grandmother," thought Little Red Riding Hood. "They will help her to get better."

So she wandered further and further from the path, gathering the prettiest of the flowers, to take to her grandmother.

By now the wolf had reached the grandmother's cottage. He knocked at the door. "Who is there?" called the grandmother.

"Little Red Riding Hood," replied the wolf. "I have brought you a cake and some wine."

"Press the latch, open the door and walk in, my dear," said Grandmother. "I am so weak that I cannot get up."

The wolf pressed the latch, opened the door and walked in. Without saying a word, he went straight to the grandmother's bed and gobbled her up in one mouthful.

Then he put on one of her nightdresses and a nightcap which he pulled well down over his eyes. He drew the curtains and got into bed, pulling the bedclothes well up to his chin. Then he waited!

Meanwhile Little Red Riding Hood had wandered far from the path, for the loveliest flowers always seemed to be furthest away.

When she had gathered so many flowers that her arms were full, she began to think again of her grandmother, lying ill in bed.

She returned to the path and went on her way.

When Little Red Riding Hood arrived at her grandmother's cottage, she was surprised to find the door standing wide open.

"Good morning, Grandmother!" she called out as she went inside, but she got no reply.

Then Little Red Riding Hood began to feel rather uneasy. She went up to the bed and drew back the curtains.

There lay her grandmother, with her cap pulled down to her eyes and the bedclothes pulled up to her chin, looking very strange.

"Oh, Grandmother!" she cried. "What big ears you have!"

"All the better to hear you with, my dear," came the reply.

"Oh, Grandmother! What big eyes you have!"

"All the better to see you with, my dear!"

"Oh, Grandmother! What big hands you have!"

"All the better to hug you with, my dear!"

"Oh, Grandmother! What a big mouth you have!"

"All the better to eat you with!"

With these words, the wolf jumped out of bed and gobbled up Little Red Riding Hood in one mouthful.

Then he climbed into bed, lay down and fell fast asleep. Soon he began to snore. He snored so loudly that the cottage shook.

Just at that time, Little Red Riding Hood's father was passing near by. He heard the awful snores coming from the cottage, and thought he had better go in to see why Little Red Riding Hood's grandmother was snoring so loudly.

When he went up to the bed, he saw the wolf lying there.

"You wicked creature!" he cried in a rage. "I have long wanted to get my hands on you!"

With one blow of his axe he killed the wolf, and pulled him out of the bed. Then he had an idea! Perhaps the wolf had swallowed the grandmother whole and perhaps he could still save her.

Then Little Red Riding Hood's father cut open the wolf, hoping to find the grandmother inside, alive.

What was his surprise when up popped a little red hood and out jumped Little Red Riding Hood!

"Oh! How frightened I was!" cried
Little Red Riding Hood. "How dark it
was inside the wolf!"

Then her father helped the grandmother
out. She was still alive but very weak.

Little Red Riding Hood and her father
put Grandmother into bed. They gave
her some of the cake and some wine.
Soon she was sitting up and feeling
much better.

How happy they all were that things had
turned out so well!

Little Red Riding Hood's father took her by the hand and led her thankfully back to her mother. And how happy *she* was that things had turned out so well!

"As long as I live," said Little Red Riding Hood to her mother, "I shall never again leave the forest path when you have warned me not to do so."